CHUGGINGTON™

SCHOLASTIC READER

LEVEL 1

50-250 WORDS

Lights, Camera, ACTION CHUGGER!

SCHOLASTIC

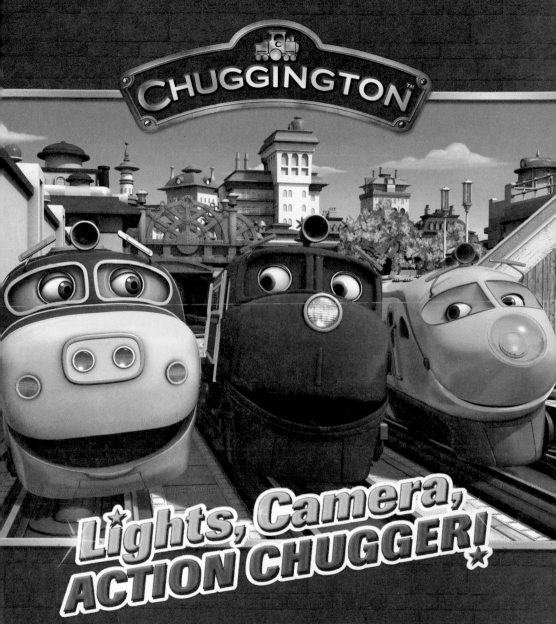

CHUGGINGTON™

Lights, Camera, ACTION CHUGGER!

Adapted by Ivy Silver
Based on the story by Sarah Ball and Jacquelyn Bell

SCHOLASTIC INC.
New York Toronto London Auckland
Sydney Mexico City New Delhi Hong Kong

ISBN 978-0-545-36857-5

12 11 10 9 8 7 6 5 4 3 2 1   12 13 14 15 16/0

Printed in the U.S.A.   40
First printing, January 2012

"Action Chugger is making a movie today," Emery says.

"I want to help make the movie!" Brewster cheers.

"Brewster, your job today is to pick up litter," Calley says.

Brewster is sad. He does not want to pick up trash.

Brewster follows Calley to the countryside.

"I wish I had a fun job," he says.

"This can be fun," Calley tells Brewster. "Look what this wagon can do!"

The wagon has a magnet.
Calley uses the magnet to pick
up a metal can.

After a few tries, Brewster can pick up a can, too!

Calley heads back to the depot.
Brewster keeps practicing.

Soon Brewster sees
Action Chugger in the sky!

Oh, no! He is in trouble!

Action Chugger lands
with a thump. He tips
off the track.

"My jet stopped working," says Action Chugger.

"I need your help!

I have some rope. Can you grab it and pull me up?"

Brewster throws his magnet.
He catches Action Chugger's
rope.

Then Brewster pulls him back on to the track.

"*Brewster to the **rescue!***" he cheers.

Then Brewster sees a branch in Action Chugger's jet. He pulls it out. "This is the reason your jet didn't work."

"Would you like to join me on my film set?"

Action Chugger flies Brewster to the film set.

Brewster is Action Chugger's special guest.

It turned out to be a fun day after all!
Lights, Camera, Action Chugger!